Ripley's Believe It or Not!®

Developed and produced by Ripley Publishing Ltd

This edition published and distributed by:

Mason Crest
370 Reed Road, Broomall, Pennsylvania 19008
www.masoncrest.com

Printed and bound in the United States of America.

First printing
9 8 7 6 5 4 3 2 1

Ripley's Believe It or Not!
Strange Sites
ISBN-13: 978-1-4222-2574-5 (hardcover)
ISBN-13: 978-1-4222-9249-5 (e-book)
Ripley's Believe It or Not!–Complete 16 Title Series
ISBN-13: 978-1-4222-2560-8

Library of Congress Cataloging-in-Publication Data

Strange sites.
     p. cm. — (Ripley's believe it or not!)
ISBN 978-1-4222-2574-5 (hardcover) — ISBN 978-1-4222-2560-8 (series hardcover) —
ISBN 978-1-4222-9249-5 (ebook)
1. Curiosities and wonders—Juvenile literature. I. Title: Strange sites.
AG243.S3983 2012
031.02—dc23
                              2012020381

PUBLISHER'S NOTE
While every effort has been made to verify the accuracy of the entries in this book, the
Publisher's cannot be held responsible for any errors contained in the work. They would
be glad to receive any information from readers.

WARNING
Some of the stunts and activities in this book are undertaken by experts and should not
be attempted by anyone without adequate training and supervision.

Ripley's Believe It or Not!®

Disbelief and Shock!

STRANGE SITES

www.MasonCrest.com

STRANGE SITES

Weird world. Find a mix of the most incredible

buildings, breathtaking landscapes, and crazy

places. Read about the upside down house, the

icebergs that are the size of a ten-story building,

and the beach in Australia that was completely

covered in white foam!

After Hurricane Ike hit Gilchrist, Texas, in 2008 this house was the only one left standing.

BANG

In the most ambitious experiment in human history, scientists have been attempting to unlock the secrets of how our universe began millions of years ago. The birth of the universe is commonly known as the Big Bang, and the scientists plan to re-create the conditions immediately after it occurred.

The ambitious experiment has been taking place 330 ft (100 m) below ground in a specially built 17-mi (27-km) circular tunnel running beneath the border between France and Switzerland. Two beams of tiny particles, called protons, are steered in opposite directions around the circuit at close to the speed of light, completing approximately 11,000 laps—a total of 187,000 mi (300,950 km)—every second. By smashing these particles together with tremendous force, scientists hope that new, even smaller particles will emerge, revealing insights into the nature of the cosmos.

Protons are found in the central part, or nucleus, of an atom. Atoms are the basic building blocks of life. They can join together to create molecules, which in turn form most of the objects around us—chairs, glass, even the air.

Hundreds of billions of protons are propelled around the tunnel so that they collide at a rate of 80 million per second. Although 200 billion protons are lined up to collide, they are so tiny—each is a trillionth the size of a mosquito—that only around 20 will actually clash. These collisions take place inside vast detectors in the tunnels and create temperatures 100,000 times hotter than the core of the Sun. Just one of the detectors weighs 13,800 tons.

The experiment, launched in September 2008, is the result of collaboration between more than 10,000 scientists and engineers from over 80 countries and 500 universities.

The 17-mi (27-km) tunnel is large enough to accommodate a passenger train.

JLG LIFTLUX 153-12

BANG!

The tunnel houses the $10-billion Large Hadron Collider, a machine called a particle accelerator. This machine uses radio waves to push beams of protons around the circuit and bunch the particles together in groups of around 100 billion. Each beam packs as much energy as a train traveling at more than 90 mph (145 km/h). At specific points around the tunnel, the beams' paths cross and they collide inside massive detectors that are ready to monitor the results of the impact and to see what is contained in the debris.

The experiment will create more than 15 million gigabytes of data every year—the equivalent of 21.4 million CDs—and took more than 13 years to build.

The central component of the Large Hadron Collider before it is placed in position.

The Large Hadron Collider stands 12 stories high and is designed to generate temperatures of more than a trillion degrees Celsius.

HIT AT SPEED OF SOUND

In 1978, at an institute in Protvino, Russia, scientific researcher Anatoli Bugorski leaned over an item of particle accelerator equipment that had malfunctioned. As he did so, his skull was penetrated by a proton beam moving at the speed of sound, causing him to be exposed to a flash of light brighter than a thousand suns and a degree of radiation 600 times greater than is usually fatal. He was expected to die within days but miraculously survived, although the entire left side of his face was paralyzed. His face was effectively divided in two. The right side continues to age normally, but the left side remains frozen in 1978. When he concentrates, he wrinkles only half his forehead.

Deer Cloud

A cloud in the shape of a reindeer graced the skies over Wellington, New Zealand. A light cirrus cloud, it formed at an altitude of around 30,000 ft (9,100 m).

MUD SLIDE ■ Mud avalanches can move at speeds in excess of 100 mph (160 km/h). On November 13, 1985, a volcano mudslide traveled 62 mi (100 km) and killed more than 23,000 people near Nevado del Ruiz, Colombia.

FISH FOSSIL ■ A stone that had sat for 15 years on an ornamental rock garden in Kent, England, was identified in 2008 as being the fossilized head of an 80-million-year-old haddock. The homeowner, Peter Parvin, had found the valuable fossil on a beach during a family holiday.

DAMAGE PATHS ■ Tornadoes can cause damage paths more than a mile (1.6 km) wide and 60 mi (96 km) long. Once a tornado in Broken Bow, Oklahoma, carried a motel sign 30 mi (48 km) and dropped it in Arkansas.

HURRICANE FORCE ■ A hurricane possesses as much energy as 10,000 nuclear bombs. A single hurricane's energy can equate to a power supply of 360 billion kilowatt hours a day—enough to supply electricity for the entire United States for six months.

EXPLOSIVE CLOUD ■ The center of our galaxy has a cloud 10,000 light years across made of antimatter, a material which explodes into pure energy on contact with normal matter.

UPLIFTING EXPERIENCE ■ An earthquake in April 2007 measuring 8.1 on the Richter scale lifted the South Pacific island of Ranongga 10 ft (3 m) higher out of the ocean.

WATER PRESSURE ■ The pressure of water on the sea floor can crush a foam cup to the size of a thimble.

MIGHTY ERUPTION ■ Io, one of Jupiter's moons, has volcanoes that erupt up to 190 mi (305 km) into the sky.

METEORITE CRATERS ■ To date, scientists have found around 200 major meteorite impact craters on Earth, ranging from dozens of feet to hundreds of miles in diameter.

LONG CANYON ■ The Valles Marineris canyon system on Mars is 3 mi (5 km) deep and 200 mi (320 km) wide in some places and is over 3,000 mi (4,830 km) long—that's long enough to stretch from California to New York.

FLOOD POWER ■ Just 6 in (15 cm) of rapidly moving flood water is enough to knock a person down.

LARGE CLOUD ■ A single cumulonimbus cloud can stretch 6 miles across and 11 miles high (10 x 18 km)—almost twice the height of Mount Everest. A large cloud can hold enough water for 500,000 baths and weigh 700,000 tons—equal to the weight of more than 110,000 full-grown elephants.

ELECTRICAL STORM ■ In 1859, a ferocious storm disconnected the batteries running the telegraph system between Portland, Oregon, and Boston, Massachusetts. The storm, however, was so powerful it generated massive natural electrical currents that enabled the telegraph system to operate as normal.

FISH FENCE

In September 2008, dozens of fish were found dead, stuck headfirst in a chain-link fence in West Orange, Texas, when the waters receded following a storm surge from Hurricane Ike.

Tornado Terror

A huge tornado funnel cloud touched down in Orchard, Iowa, in June 2008. A witness said the funnel spiraled down close to the ground before going back up into the clouds.

NEARLY FRIED ■ Dave Fern of Pueblo, Colorado, was frying a tortilla in his home in 2001 when lightning struck a tree in his yard and traveled down a power line to his stove, burning a hole in his frying pan.

METEORITE MALAISE ■ A meteorite that crashed in Peru in September 2007—creating a crater 15 ft (4.5 m) deep and 65 ft (20 m) wide —apparently caused headaches, vomiting, and nausea among dozens of local people.

NARROW BOLT ■ Although the length of a lightning bolt can be as much as 5 mi (8 km), its diameter is usually between just ½ in and 1 in (1.2 cm and 2.5 cm).

HERDERS RESCUED ■ Two reindeer herders were rescued in 2005 after being buried under snow for six days following an avalanche in Kamchatka, Russia.

RAPID REBUILD ■ When a tornado destroyed Chris Graber's home in Marshfield, Missouri, in 2006, his Amish neighbors helped him build a new one in fewer than 15 hours.

POSITIVE GIANTS ■ Some lightning strikes hit the ground up to 20 mi (32 km) away from the storm—and because they appear to strike from a clear sky they are referred to as "bolts from the blue." Known as "Positive Giants," these flashes carry several times the destructive energy of a normal lightning strike.

ACE VACUUM ■ A person exposed to the vacuum of space will fall unconscious after about 15 seconds, but is likely to survive a minute or two with little permanent effect.

COLLISION COURSE ■ The Martian moon Phobos orbits less than 6,000 mi (9,660 km) from Mars. Within 50 million years, it will either crash into the planet or break apart.

LIGHT SATURN ■ With the smallest density of any planet in the Solar System, Saturn is so light that it could float on water—if there were an ocean large enough to accommodate it!

RAPID ACCELERATION ■ An avalanche of snow can reach a speed of 80 mph (130 km/h) within five seconds after it fractures away from the mountainside.

QUAKE DAMAGE ■ There are 500,000 detectable earthquakes each year. Of these, 100,000 can be felt, but only 100 cause damage.

WEATHER EXTREMES ■ In the first half of 2007, floods, landslides, and mudslides triggered by torrential rain killed 652 people in China and destroyed 452,000 homes. At the same time, nearly one million people in the country's Jiangxi Province were suffering shortages of drinking water after a month-long drought.

SPACE JUNK ■ More than 6,000 tons of man-made items, including more than 200 derelict satellites, are floating in orbit above our planet.

Ripley's research

Swept inland as the area flooded and water levels rose alarmingly, the fish were swimming along in the swollen waters until they came to a fence and, being up to 10 in (25 cm) long, were too big to get through. Many of the fish were still stuck in the 4-ft-high (1.2-m) fence two days later.

FOAM BATH

In August 2007, bathers in the sea at Yamba, Australia, found themselves in what looked like a giant bubble bath, when thick sea foam started to wash in on the beach. This rare phenomenon is not fully explained, but it is thought to be caused by elements in the sea, such as microscopic organisms, dead fish, and seaweed, being churned to a froth by large waves as they near the shore. The foam at Yamba was thought to extend 165 ft (50 m) out to sea.

IGUANA FALL ■ An unusual night of cold weather in January 2008 caused dozens of chilled iguanas to drop unconscious out of trees in Key Biscayne, Florida.

LIGHTNING STRIKE ■ A three-year-old boy slept through a lightning strike in May 2008 that sounded like "a massive explosion" and blew a hole in his bedroom wall. The lightning blew all the lightbulbs and electrical equipment in the house in Flint, North Wales, but, remarkably, Elis Roberts remained fast asleep in his room, even though it was covered in masonry, plaster, and dust.

RODE AVALANCHE ■ A veteran ski patroller from New Zealand survived an avalanche in 2007 by riding down it for more than 1,200 ft (365 m). He was finally buried by the snow, which carried him an additional 500 ft (150 m), but he managed to dig himself out with the help of two companions.

EXPLODING TOILETS ■ Hundreds of thousands of hailstones suddenly exploded out of toilets in an Austrian apartment block in July 2008, forcing startled residents to flee the building. One man, who was sitting on a toilet at the time, was blasted off it as the avalanche of ice quickly filled the entire building. The freak incident—at Eisenstadt—was caused by hailstones flooding into and blocking a local drain during a torrential downpour.

COAL FALL ■ In 1983, lumps of coke and coal mysteriously fell out of the sky and landed on yachtsmen in Poole Harbour, Dorset, England.

VALUABLE METEORITES ■ For many years, the standard price for meteoritic material was $1 per pound, but now many meteorites are worth as much as gold. Unsuspecting finders have used fallen meteorites as such things as blacksmith anvils and dog bowls, and for propping up autos.

BELL DEATH ■ Jean Rugibet of Trouille, France, rushed to the local belfry during a lightning storm in 1807 to prove that his beloved bells could drive away bad weather. The storm passed but the bells continued to ring, and friends found his body, fused by lightning to the bell ropes.

BEACH GARBAGE ■ In July 2007, a shift in ocean currents began dumping up to 300 tons of floating garbage every day on the Juhu Beach area near Mumbai, India.

FOSSILIZED FOREST ■ While digging for lignite, or brown coal, in 2007, miners in northeastern Hungary discovered an eight-million-year-old swamp cypress forest. Sixteen fossilized trees were found—the tallest around 20 ft (6 m)—and, amazingly, they had not petrified, or turned to stone, as preserved trees usually do—instead, they had retained their original wood.

Branching Out

These incredible trees are specially grafted to grow into sophisticated shapes by Peter and Becky Cook of Queensland, Australia. Peter once wondered if he could grow a chair and, over many years, his idea came to fruition. The Cooks meticulously plan all their creations, and among their shaped living trees are action figures that have green leaves sprouting from their heads as hair, and the amazing living wooden chair that is strong enough to support a fully grown man.

A Cut Above

Trimming the biggest hedge in Britain is a tall job, and it takes gardener Peter Pidgley a week to tidy up each side. The yew hedge grows in Dorset, England, and was planted during the reign of King Edward VI in the 16th century. The work creates a huge pile of cuttings, but the cuttings don't go to waste—they are sent to France to be used in the development of anti-cancer drugs.

GLOBAL DANGER ■ More than one million species of plants and animals—a quarter of all life on land—could become extinct in just decades as a result of man-made climate change. Australia alone could lose more than half of its 400-plus butterfly species by 2050.

MIRACLE BERRY ■ Known also as the miracle fruit, the berry of *Synsepalum dulcificum* creates a chemical reaction that raises your sense of sweetness, making lemons taste like candy, beer taste like chocolate and hot sauce taste like donut glaze. The effect lasts for about an hour. The berry is native to West Africa, but is now being harvested in South Florida where a single berry sells for $3.

ANCIENT SEED ■ Botanists in Israel have managed to germinate a seed that is 2,000 years old. The 5-ft-tall (1.5-ft) Judean date palm was grown from the seed of a date eaten by Jewish rebels who once occupied the Roman garrison at Masada. The seed was discovered in a jar of discarded date pits during excavations of Masada in the 1960s.

Tree Wheel

A Phoenix tree in China has an unusual growth: a bicycle wheel rim. According to locals in Mengcheng Town, Anhui Province, a bicycle repairman used to ply his trade nearby and nailed the rim to the tree as an advertisement. Over the years, the tree grew around the wheel, which now looks as if it has been there forever.

SPACE DUST ■ Every day around 40 tons of space dust enter the atmosphere and fall to the Earth's surface—that's the equivalent of the weight of eight African elephants.

OLD SPRUCE ■ A spruce tree root system in Sweden has been sprouting new trees for nearly 10,000 years. Scientists think the tree in Dalarna originally took root around the year 7542 BC.

WATER FORCE ■ Tsunami waves travel across oceans at speeds of up to 500 mph (800 km/h). Waves hitting coastlines have shifted 20-ton rocks hundreds of yards inland.

IN THE DARK ■ On September 28, 2006, street lights across Iceland were shut off to give citizens a better view of the stars—while an astronomer explained what they were seeing over the country's national radio station.

25-HOUR DAYS? ■ Because of the Earth's decelerating rotation, in the future days may have 25 hours. A British astronomer has proved the Earth's spin has been slowing down since 700 BC.

Out in Space...

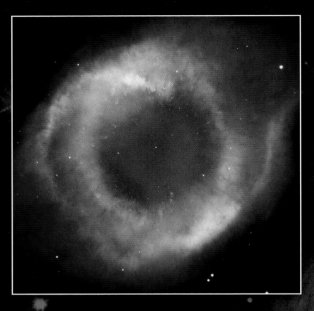

Snapping stunning photographs of galaxies millions of miles from Earth is the job of the Hubble Space Telescope, launched in 1990 at a cost of $1.5 billion, and named after the U.S. astronomer Edwin Hubble.

From its position in orbit some 353 mi (568 km) above the Earth, the camera is free from the Earth's atmosphere, giving it a far better view of space than telescopes on Earth despite moving at 17,500 mph (27,358 km/h). The telescope has sent many thousands of pictures back to Earth, and each week produces enough data to fill 3,600 ft (1,097 m) of books on a bookshelf.

Helix Nebula

NASA used nine different pictures taken by both the Hubble Space Telescope and a telescope in Tucson, Arizona, to produce this photograph of the Helix Nebula, because the nebula (an enormous cloud of dust and gas) is too big for one camera to capture. Formed from gases expelled by a dying star, like our Sun, it is 690 light years away— this means that light from the nebula takes 690 years to reach Earth, traveling a whopping 4,000 trillion Earth miles.

Sombrero Galaxy

The "Sombrero Galaxy" is so-called because it is shaped like the famous Mexican hat. What looks like a solid band of rock is actually a ring of space dust and, with its brilliantly bright core, it can be seen with small telescopes from Earth. It is 800 billion times the size of our Sun, 50,000 light years across—one light year is equivalent to about 5.8 trillion miles (9.3 trillion km)—and has a massive black hole in it. The galaxy is about 28 million light years away from Earth, and is estimated to be hurtling away from us at a speed of 700 miles per second (1,126 km per second) owing to the expansion of the universe.

SPACE FACTS

> The Earth orbits the Sun, a star, which is the center of our Solar System. Our Solar System is one of possibly billions that lie in our galaxy, the Milky Way. There are at least 200 billion stars in the Milky Way, which, in turn, is one of more than 100 billion possible galaxies in the known universe.

> Each year more than 14,000 tons of cosmic dust fall to Earth—that's equivalent to the weight of more than 3,000 African elephants.

> Our galaxy, the Milky Way, is 100,000 light years wide. In Earth miles, this is almost 600 quadrillion, or 600 thousand million million, miles. This means that if you traveled at 100 mph (161 km/h) it would take more than 600,000,000,000 years—600 billion—to get to the other side.

> We can see only 0.000002 percent, or around 2,500, of the stars in the Milky Way with the naked eye from any fixed point on the Earth.

Whirlpool

The Whirlpool Galaxy features "arms" of stars and gas laced with space dust. The galaxy is 31 million light years away from Earth.

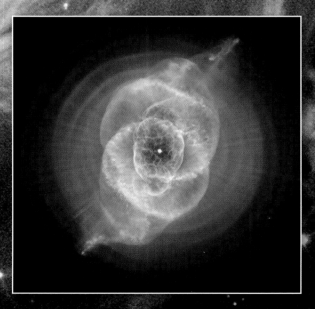

Cat's Eye Nebula

Like a great eye peering from a distant galaxy, the Cat's Eye Nebula was one of the first to be seen, more than 200 years ago, and can be found 3,300 light years from Earth. This particular nebula features dust rings in a circular pattern. Each ring of dust is thought to contain as much mass as all the planets in our Solar System combined.

Red Supergiant

A red supergiant star 20,000 light years away from Earth suddenly brightened for a few weeks— becoming 600,000 times brighter than our Sun. The Hubble Space Telescope caught the results some two years later as dust swirled around the star at the center, like the flash of a camera itself.

ICE MASS ■ Iceberg B15, which broke off from the Ross Ice Shelf in Antarctica in 2000, measured an amazing 183 mi (295 km) long and 23 mi (37 km) wide and weighed about 3 billion tons. Covering around 11,000 sq mi (28,500 sq km), it was approximately twice the size of the state of Delaware.

DISTANT FORCES ■ Iceberg B15 broke apart in 2002 and the largest remaining piece of it, B15-A, split up in 2005, its demise caused by an ocean swell generated by an Alaskan storm that took place six days earlier and over 8,000 mi (12,875 km) away.

WATER SUPPLY ■ An iceberg that broke free from Antarctica in 1987 weighed around 1.4 trillion tons and could have supplied everyone in the world with half a gallon (2 l) of water a day for 330 years.

TOURIST ATTRACTION ■ An iceberg that floated past New Zealand's South Island in 2006 became a tourist attraction. People paid $330 a person to fly over the unusual iceberg, the first to be visible from the New Zealand shore since 1931.

LONG JOURNEY ■ An iceberg once floated an amazing 2,500 mi (4,000 km) all the way from the Arctic to Bermuda—without melting.

MONUMENTAL 'BERG ■ Although only one-eighth of an iceberg actually lies visible above the waterline, an iceberg in the north Atlantic Ocean stood an incredible 550 ft (168 m) tall—almost the height of the Washington Monument. By contrast, the iceberg that famously sank the cruise liner *Titanic* in 1912 measured just 75 ft (23 m) above the surface of the water.

SHIPWRECK RESCUE ■ In 1875, the schooner *Caledonia* was wrecked 9 mi (14.5 km) off Newfoundland, Canada, but her crew of 82 survived by climbing onto an iceberg so that they could be rescued.

SINGING ICEBERGS ■ A team of German scientists has discovered that some icebergs can sing. The sounds, which resemble the violin section of an orchestra, are too low to be heard by humans, but have been picked up by seismic recordings. They occur during an iceberg tremor, when water squeezes through the iceberg's crevasses, forcing the walls to shake.

QUICK MELT ■ An iceberg 80 ft (24 m) high and 300 ft (91 m) long would melt in 70°F (21°C) weather in only four days.

'BERG SPEED ■ The average speed of icebergs off Newfoundland, Canada, is 0.4 mph (0.7 km/h), although with favorable conditions they have been observed moving at up to 2.2 mph (3.6 km/h)—nearly as fast as a human can walk.

AIRCRAFT CARRIERS ■ During World War II, British scientist Geoffrey Pyke came up with the idea of using icebergs as aircraft carriers, thinking they would be impossible to sink. Although a model was built in 1943 on Patricia Lake, Alberta, Canada, the secret plan (code-named "Habbakuk") was scrapped because the ice split too easily.

Icebergs don't just come in white, as these photographs from the Antarctic prove spectacularly. Nor are they uniformly "mini-mountain" in size and appearance.

Rather, icebergs can vary from being the size of a small car—these are called "growlers"—to icy formations that have the dimensions of a ten-story building. Familiar shapes include pinnacle 'bergs (with one or more spires), domes (rounded top), wedges (a steep edge on one side with a slope on the opposite side) and blocky 'bergs (steep, vertical sides with a flat top).

However, some of the most spectacular icebergs are actually striped, like giant candies. These stripes are often formed by layers of snow that melt and refreeze, and the stark colorings can be the result of more than a thousand years of shaping and compacting by the ice. Blue stripes are created when a crevice in the ice sheet fills up with melted water and freezes so quickly that no bubbles form. Other stripes are created from dust and soil picked up when the ice sheet from which the iceberg comes grinds downhill toward the sea. As ice crystals form a new layer at the base of the shelf, the resultant stripes can be black, brown or yellow or, if the trapped sediment is rich in algae, green. The stripes then move through the structure as it changes shape in the water to create stunning effects.

INCREDIBLE ICEBERGS

BASKET BLOCK ■ The Longaberger Company of Newark, Ohio, has its head office built in the shape of one of its trademark wicker baskets. The seven-story building is topped with two huge metal handles, each weighing 75 tons.

MOTOR HOME ⊠ Auto-mad architect Dan Scully built his New Hampshire home in the shape of a car, complete with two round windows as headlights and the bumper from a Volkswagen bus. Inside, old car seats provide Dan with his furniture.

STRING HALL ■ The Chowdiah Memorial Hall in Bangalore, India, is built in the shape of a giant violin to honor master violinist Tirumakudalu Chowdiah.

MUSICAL HIGHWAY ■ A strip of road in Lancaster, California, plays the "William Tell Overture" when cars drive over it at 55 mph (88 km/h). The notes were created by workers carving grooves into the road surface.

HOUSE IN THE COOKIE JAR ■ Built in 1947, a three-story house in Glendora, New Jersey, is shaped like a cookie jar.

ELEPHANT RESTAURANT ■ Formerly a restaurant and tavern, Lucy the elephant is now a historic landmark in Margate, New Jersey. The 90-ton elephant-shaped building was hit by lightning in 2006, leaving Lucy's tusks blackened.

LIVES IN A SHOE ■ In Bakersfield, California, there stands a shoe-repair shop that is built in the shape of a 30-ft-long (9-m), 20-ft-high (6-m) shoe, complete with chain laces.

ROBOTIC BANK ■ The 20-story Bank of Asia building in Bangkok, Thailand, is shaped like a giant robot, and even has two 20-ft-high (6-m) lidded "eyes" that serve as windows on the top floor. The eyeballs are made of glass and the lids are metal louvers.

DOG-SHAPED INN ■ The Dog Bark Park Inn at Cottonwood, Idaho, is a bed-and-breakfast establishment built in the shape of a giant beagle.

HAVING A BALL ■ Dutch architect Jan Sonkie is such a keen soccer fan that he built his four-story house in Blantyre, Malawi, in the shape of a soccer ball.

SOMETHING FISHY ■ The National Freshwater Fishing Hall of Fame Museum in Hayward, Wisconsin, is housed in a building 143 ft (43.5 m) long shaped like a muskie fish.

MOTHER GOOSE HOUSE ■ A building in Hazard, Kentucky, is shaped like a goose sitting on its nest. The giant bird's head and neck form the roof, while the windows below are egg-shaped.

BOAT WASH ■ A car wash at Eau Claire, Wisconsin, is shaped like a cruise liner, right down to its two smoke stacks.

KEEP ROLLING ■ An optical illusion created by undulating terrain means that cars amazingly appear to roll uphill at Magnetic Hill, near Moncton, New Brunswick, Canada.

BARKING MAD ■ Barking Sands Beach on the Hawaiian island of Kauai has sand that barks like a dog. The dry sand grains emit the strange sound when people walk on them in bare feet.

DUCK WALKWAY ■ So many carp gather at the base of the spillway of the Pymatuning Reservoir, Linesville, Pennsylvania, that ducks walk across the backs of the fish and hardly get their feet wet.

SHARP TURNS ■ The road to Hana on the Hawaiian island of Maui is 52 mi (84 km) long but has over 600 hairpin bends—that's 12 sharp turns every mile, or one every 150 yd (137 m).

BEHIND THE TIMES ■ Churches in Malta have two clocks showing different times. One is correct but the other is deliberately wrong in order to confuse the devil about the time of the next service.

ETERNAL FLAME ■ A burning seam of coal that lies 500 ft (152 m) below the surface in the Hunter Valley, New South Wales, Australia, creates a continuous column of smoke from the fire that never goes out.

NO CARS ALLOWED ■ Juneau, the state capital of Alaska, can be reached only by water or air, because there are no roads leading to the city.

GREAT GUST ■ A three-second gust of wind during a tornado near Oklahoma City, Oklahoma, on May 3, 1999, reached a speed of over 300 mph (483 km/h).

ROCKS AND STRIPES

Sandstone rock at Coyote Butte on the border between Arizona and Utah makes stunning natural waves and stripes. The distinctive patterns were formed as light sand piled up with heavier sand and grit over millions of years, eventually becoming compacted into rock and eroded into smooth waves.

How long do you think you can hold your breath? Imagine diving down an incredible 702 ft (214 m) into the ocean with no breathing apparatus and only fish for company! This is what free diver Herbert Nitsch from Austria did. A champion in the extreme sport of free diving, Herbert dived to this depth in Spetses, Greece, in June 2008, using only the air in his lungs.

Herbert used a weighted sled on the way down, in order to reach this depth. While still in relatively shallow water, he used a soda bottle to help equalize the pressure in his ears, but as he went deeper he had only his own intense training techniques to prevent him from passing out.

As the water pressure increases, Herbert's lungs can shrink to the size of a fist, the blood vessels there eventually flooding with blood to stop the chest cavity from collapsing as the pressure at 656 ft (200 m) reaches almost 300 lb (136 kg) per square inch. The entire Spetses dive took 4 minutes 24 seconds. Descending at a rate of 10 ft 6 in (3.2 m) per second, it took him 1 minute 45 seconds to reach this incredible depth, where he waited three seconds before ascending with the aid of a rope at a speed of 13 ft (4 m) per second.

Safety precautions are vital in the dangerous sport of free diving—when he is deep enough, Herbert removes the nose clip to flood his sinuses with water.

Descending into the depths, Herbert is helped downward by a heavy-weighted sled.

A bulbous "helmet" helps to improve Herbert's hydrodynamics.

Herbert is meticulous in his preparation for a dive and tests all of his equipment carefully.

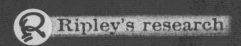

Ripley's research

Surprisingly, it is not at crushing depths that free divers are in most danger, but just before they resurface. Fit and healthy athletes can succumb to unconsciousness with no warning as the brain finally becomes starved of oxygen.

The air pressure underwater means that the human body loses its buoyancy at only 32 ft (10 m) down and the lungs shrink to half their size. When a free diver drops below 100 ft (30 m), the lungs shrink again to about the size of an orange. Below 328 ft (100 m), some divers counteract painful water pressure by actually flooding the sinus passages in their head. At this point, the heart rate can drop below 20 beats per minute (the normal rate is about 70). An extreme phenomenon observed in super-deep dives is that the body allows blood to pass into organs to keep pressure from literally squashing vital organs; for example, the shrunken lungs are flooded. Some have warned that this means that extreme free divers who sink too deep are at risk of drowning not in seawater but their own blood, should these blood vessels burst under the pressure.

TREE HOUSE

This Christmas tree in a house in the town of Bournemouth, England, appears to start on the ground floor and go straight up through the roof. In fact, it is an illusion created by the owner, Greig Howe, who bought a 35-ft (10.6-m) tree and sawed it into three sections before placing the trunk in the living room, the middle in a spare bedroom and the top on a flat roof. He did this to impress his son Harry, who thought that the previous year's 5-ft (1.5-m) tree was a bit small.

TILTING TOWERS ■ Completed in 2008, the 768-ft-high (234-m) China Central Television Center in Beijing tilts at an angle of ten degrees—almost twice the deviation of the Leaning Tower of Pisa. The steel-and-glass building has been designed in a series of L-shapes to enable it to withstand an earthquake measuring eight on the Richter scale. The building's two towers are connected at their summit by a right-angled bridge—an operation so delicate that it had to be carried out at 4 a.m. when the metal was at its coolest, to avoid the possibility of expansion.

DOLLAR HOUSE ■ A two-story house in Detroit, Michigan, sold for $1 in August 2008. The abandoned house, described as "the nicest on the block" when it sold for $65,000 in November 2006, was reduced to a bargain price as a result of the U.S. housing market crash.

HIDDEN SKELETONS ■ A house in Chicago, Illinois, changed hands three times between 2006 and 2008 before someone finally examined a bedroom and discovered the skeletons of a man and his dog.

CHURCH CONVERSION ■ A Chicago real estate agent converted his $3-million home into a church in 2007. George Michael placed a cross on the side of his lakeside mansion and renamed it the American Church of Lake Bluff, holding services there for a handful of friends and family after acquiring a pastor's degree on the Internet.

SUMMER EXPANSION ■ Paris's famous Eiffel Tower grows up to 7 in (17 cm) in height each year in summer because the sun's heat causes an expansion of the iron from which the landmark is made.

PLANE ON ROOF ■ In Abuja, Nigeria, there is a two-story concrete house with a replica of a jet aircraft embedded in the roof, as if it has landed there. The plane on the roof is 100 ft (30 m) long and 20 ft (6 m) high at the top of its tail and was built by Said Jammal to please his wife Liza who loves airplanes. He hopes to build a kitchen inside the fuselage.

FOREIGN ACCENT ■ The entire population of the tiny Pacific island of Palmerston Atoll in the Cook Islands speaks with an accent from England's West Country—12,000 mi (19,300 km) away. That's because all 63 inhabitants are descended from William Marsters, a Gloucestershire carpenter and barrel-maker who settled on the island in 1863 and who had four wives, 17 children and 54 grandchildren.

BLOOMING BIG ■ The Aalsmeer Flower Auction House in the Netherlands is so big that it covers more than 125 football fields. Eighty percent of the world's cut flowers pass through it each day, a total of 3.5 billion flowers a year.

HONEY DRIP ■ So many bees live in the walls of a stately Tudor home in San Marino, California, that honey drips out of the walls. Thousands—maybe millions—of bees have been sharing the house with Helen and Jerry Stathatos for more than 20 years, discoloring the wallpaper in the dining room and making the whole house smell sweet, like a jar of honey.

CHEEK TO CHEEK ■ The Miniscule of Sound, a nightclub measuring just 4 x 8 ft (1.2 x 2.4 m) in Hackney, London, England, holds only 14 people—including the D.J. Located in the changing booth of a disused outdoor swimming pool, it has a dance floor of 20 sq ft (1.8 sq m) and comes complete with mirror ball.

SMOKE HOLES ■ Following a ban on smoking indoors, Michael Windisch, owner of the Maltermeister Turm Bar in Goslar, Germany, cut holes in his exterior wall so that his customers could lean out and smoke without going outside.

PLAIN OF JARS ■ Scattered around the fields of Xieng Khouang Province in Laos are thousands of stone jars up to 10 ft (3 m) tall. The jars, each of which can weigh as much as 14 tons, lie in clusters, with up to 250 at an individual site. Archeologists believe the jars date back at least 1,500 years and may have been used as funeral urns or to store food.

ROOF GARDEN ■ Designed by Viennese architect Friedensreich Hundertwasser, the Waldspirale apartment building in Darmstadt, Germany, has a roof completely covered with vegetation and also has more than 1,000 windows, each of which is unique.

House Spider

A spider that was as big as a house appeared on the side of a building in Liverpool, England, in September 2008. Made from steel and wood, the 50-ft (15-m), French-designed, mechanical spider was suspended from the building as a work of art. Weighing 37 tons, the giant arachnid—called La Princess—had sophisticated hydraulics that enabled the dozen engineers strapped to its frame to operate its eyes, legs and abdomen so that it could also crawl along the streets at 2 mph (3.2 km/h).

OXYGEN CHAMBER ■ The lower house of the Japanese legislature has an oxygen booth in which tired legislators can refresh themselves.

MOVING HOUSE ■ Tim and Jennifer O'Farrell bought a house in the United States—and then had it shipped to Canada. The 3,360-sq-ft (312-sq-m), two-story waterfront house made a two-day, 280-mi (450-km) journey from Hunts Point, Washington, to its new location across the border on Vancouver Island, British Columbia, by barge. The previous owners had bought the Lake Washington property for $9.4 million in 2007 but wanted only the land, not the house.

LOCKER HOME ■ A German man slept in a lost-and-found luggage locker at a railway station for nine years. Every evening, Mike Konrad climbed feet-first into locker 501 at Düsseldorf station, squeezing his body into the space, 31 x 2 ft (9.5 x 0.6 m), usually reserved for passengers' suitcases. He always left the door ajar while he slept, so that he could obtain a refund on the $3 he had to pay to open the locker.

DIFFERENT TONGUES ■ The tiny Pacific island nation of Vanuatu has only 210,000 people but 110 indigenous languages.

WOODEN SKYSCRAPER ■ A log cabin in Arkhangelsk, Russia, rises 144 ft (44 m) above the ground and has 13 floors. When Nikolai Sutyagin began work on the wooden skyscraper in 1992, he added just three floors, but he then decided it looked ungainly so he added another and then just kept going...

BARGAIN BRIDGE ■ A steel bridge in Soldiers Grove, Wisconsin, was put up for sale for $1 in 2007. The defunct Kickapoo River Bridge was built in 1910 but hadn't carried traffic since 1976 because of its deteriorating condition.

HIGH LIFE ■ The blood of people living on the 3-mi-high (4.8-km) Tibetan Plateau is pumped through their bodies at twice the rate of lowlanders.

Fancy a Dip?

A swimming pool at a resort in Algrarrobo, near Santiago, Chile, is so huge that small boats often sail in it. The pool, which took five years to build, measures 3,323 ft (1,013 m) long, covers 20 acres (8 ha), and holds 66 million gallons of water—and the water is so clear you can see the bottom, even at the 115-ft (35-m) deep end.

LUCKY NUMBER ■ Federal Hill, a plantation house in Bardstown, Kentucky, was built with 13 front windows, 13 steps on its stairs, 13 mantles, 13-ft-high (4-m) ceilings, and 13-in-thick (33-cm) walls.

LOST LANGUAGE ■ The last two people in the world who speak the Apayan Zoque language of Apayan, Tabasco, Mexico, are two men in their seventies, who refuse to speak to each other.

TREE HOUSE ■ David Csaky spent two years living in a tree house in Seattle, Washington. He lived 30 ft (9 m) above the ground on a 300-sq-ft (28-sq-m) self-made platform, which was accessible by a ladder counter-weighted with sandbags on pulleys. He fitted his tree house with a tent, wood stove, three chairs, shelves, and a counter and shared it with various pets, including a rat, a ferret, and a squirrel.

DOG CEMETERY ■ Tuscambia, Alabama, has a cemetery that is reserved exclusively for raccoon hunting dogs.

LAST SPEAKER ■ Eighty-three-year-old Soma Devi Dura of Nepal is the last fluent speaker of the Dura language on the planet. To communicate with her husband, children, and grandchildren, she has to use other languages.

OLDEST BEEHIVES ■ Archeologists in Israel have found beehives that are around 3,000 years old. The discoveries in the ruins of the city of Rehov are thought to be the oldest intact beehives ever located.

ISLAND SALE ■ The owners of the European Channel Island of Herm, which measures 1.5 mi (2.4 km) long and 0.5 mi (0.8 km) wide, and has a population of just 50, put the entire island up for sale in 2008 at a price of $30 million.

CONCRETE TREE ■ Architect Madame Hang Nga has designed a guesthouse in the resort of Da Lat, southern Vietnam, which looks like a tree but is actually made of concrete. The five-roomed residence is known locally as the Crazy House.

FIRST CONTACT ■ The Metyktire tribe, located in a remote area of the Brazilian Amazon some 1,200 mi (1,930 km) from Rio de Janeiro, made its first contact with the outside world in May 2007. The isolation ended when two Metyktire members suddenly appeared in the village of a neighboring tribe.

STEPFATHER INCLUDED ■ An apartment was put up for sale in a sought-after district of Stockholm, Sweden, in August 2008—complete with live-in stepfather. The woman who inherited a share of the apartment after her mother died wanted to sell it, but her stepfather refused to move out.

BOARD FENCE

Hawaiian Donald "D.J." Dettloff is a surfer with a big imagination. Almost 20 years ago, with a storm threatening Maui, he tied his surfboards up with wire to prevent them from being blown away, giving him the inspiration for what has become a local landmark—a fence made entirely of surfboards. Over the years it has grown to include 700 boards, with many donated by friends and strangers, who all wanted to contribute their own surfboards, body boards, and kite boards to the fence.

MAUI
SURFBOARD FENCE
KA'OHU FA' IS PE'AHI

MAIL BACKLOG ■ Owing to the country's 2002–07 civil war, Ivory Coast's postal service had a five-year backlog of undelivered mail.

CAVE NETWORK ■ The Mammoth Cave National Park in Kentucky houses more than 367 mi (590 km) of caves—longer than the distance between Los Angeles and San Francisco—and the figure is growing each year as new passageways are discovered.

ONLY OFFICER ■ Malcolm Gilbert is the first and only full-time police officer on Pitcairn Island in the South Pacific. The nearest police backup is in New Zealand, which lies 3,300 mi (5,310 km) away.

NO CAPITAL ■ Along with Tokelau and Western Sahara, the South Pacific island of Nauru is one of only three countries in the world without an official capital. Its government offices are all situated in the Yaren District, but no single place has been designated as capital.

HUMAN ROOTS ■ New research has revealed that humans originated from a single point in central Africa. Scientists from Cambridge University, England, studied more than 6,000 skulls of indigenous people from all over the world and concluded that modern humankind developed around Africa's Great Rift Valley.

NOISE ANNOYS ■ The town of Tilburg in the Netherlands has begun issuing 5,000 euro ($6,800) fines to a local Catholic priest for ringing his church bells too loudly when he calls worshipers for early morning Mass.

BUBBLE HOUSE ■ High above Nice, France, in Tourette-sur-Loup sits a home known as the Bubble House. Designed by Antti Lovag, it consists of a series of connected bubble-shaped rooms covered in oval, convex windows and set into the volcanic rock hillside.

Baobab Bar

This enormous Baobab tree is in Limpopo province, South Africa, and stands 72 ft (22 m) high with an incredible 154 ft (47 m) circumference. It is so large that a bar big enough for 60 people has been installed inside the trunk, and there's room for plenty more outside! Baobab trees become naturally hollow over time, and the bar tree in Limpopo has been dated at more than 6,000 years old.

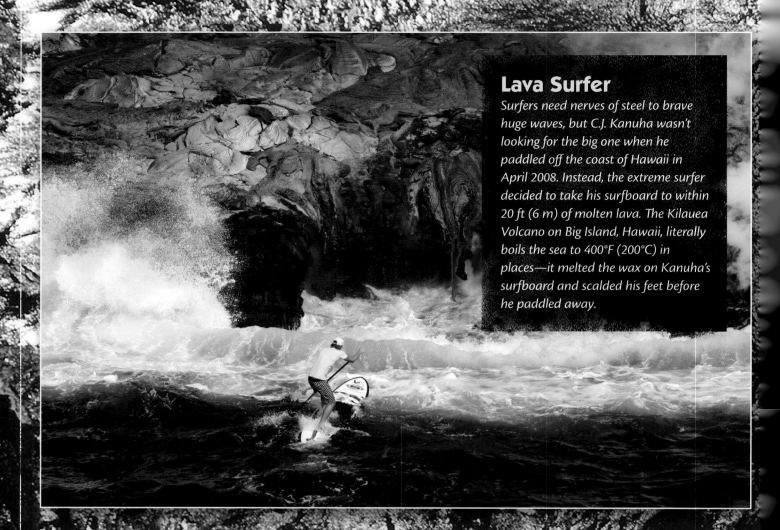

Lava Surfer

Surfers need nerves of steel to brave huge waves, but C.J. Kanuha wasn't looking for the big one when he paddled off the coast of Hawaii in April 2008. Instead, the extreme surfer decided to take his surfboard to within 20 ft (6 m) of molten lava. The Kilauea Volcano on Big Island, Hawaii, literally boils the sea to 400°F (200°C) in places—it melted the wax on Kanuha's surfboard and scalded his feet before he paddled away.

Heads Up

Sri-Lankan-born surfer Dulip Kokuhannadige is trying to start a topsy-turvy craze riding waves off the south coast of England—surfing on his head for as long as 15 seconds at a time. He discovered the new style when teaching young people to surf in the aftermath of the 2004 tsunami, in which he lost all his possessions, and took the upside-down idea to England when he moved to the coastal town of Bournemouth a year later.

WHALE SCARE

Kiteboarder David Sheridan was 300 ft (100 m) from shore off New South Wales, Australia, when he noticed a dark shape loom from the depths. A Southern Right Whale wacked him in the back of the head with its tail, almost knocking him off his board, but luckily for Sheridan from Nambucca, it is thought that the huge whale was just issuing a warning.

Sole Survivor

When Hurricane Ike battered the town of Gilchrist, Texas, in 2008, it flattened everything in its path—except for the house of Warren and Pam Adams. It remained the last house standing because it was built on 14-ft-high (4.3-m) wooden columns. The Adams family had learned their lesson in 2005 when their previous home was destroyed by Hurricane Rita.

FAST MOVER ■ Vanda James from Great Yarmouth, England, has moved house a staggering 27 times in four years. Her quest for the ideal home—it included a three-month stay in New Zealand—has seen her move on average once every eight weeks and spend some $60,000 on deposits and removal fees plus 648 hours packing and unpacking. Her shortest stay in a house was one week. "It just didn't feel right," she says.

COMPACT HOME ■ Dee Williams lives in a house in Olympia, Washington, that is no bigger than a parking spot. She built the 84 sq ft (7.8 sq m) cabin herself out of salvaged material and now it sits in her friend's backyard. Two solar panels provide electricity and it takes Dee just four paces to get from one end of her house to the other.

TOWERING LOVE ■ A woman from San Francisco is married to the Eiffel Tower. Erika La Tour Eiffel (she changed her name to cement her union with the French monument) has a condition that causes her to form relationships with inanimate objects rather than people. She is also in love with the Golden Gate Bridge.

28

Spaceship House

A house in Chattanooga, Tennessee, that is shaped like a flying saucer was sold at auction in 2008 for a down-to-earth bid of $135,000. Built in 1970, shortly after the first Moon landing, the mountainside dwelling has small square windows, directional lights and is perched on six "landing gear" legs. It also has a retractable staircase at the entrance.

UPSIDE DOWN
UPSIDE DOWN

A house with a difference was unveiled to the public at Trassenheide, northern Germany, in 2008—because both the outside and inside are upside down. Visitors to the house, which was designed by Polish architects Klausdiusz Golos and Sebastian Mikiciuk, reported feeling dizzy as they encountered chairs, tables and carpets that had been stuck to the ceiling to create the inverted interior and give people an alternative view of everyday items.

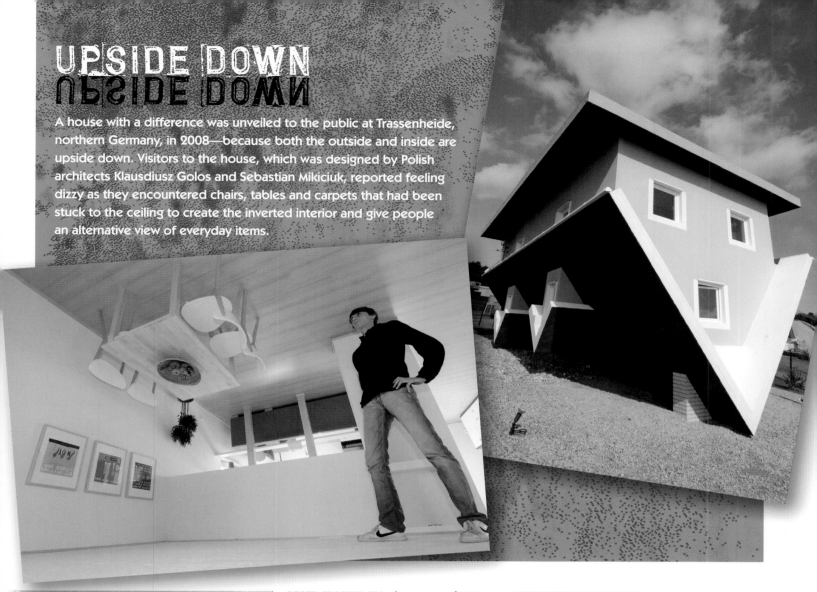

DONKEY LAW ■ South Shields, England, has had a law on the books for 800 years allowing city officials to block construction of any market that is within a day's ride by donkey—and, incredibly, it's still enforced!

HOUSE STOLEN ■ Yuri Konstantinov from Astrakhan, Russia, returned from a holiday in 2008 to discover that his entire two-story house had been stolen. A neighbor had taken down the building brick by brick and sold all the contents.

TIN MAN ■ In a protest against bureaucracy, Geoff Harper of Scorton, North Yorkshire, England, added a 30-ft (9-m) Tin Man to the exterior of his house, choosing his subject because, in his view, the local council, like the Tin Man from *The Wizard of Oz*, had no heart.

ESTATE CONDITIONS ■ Hélène Louart of Pellevoisin, France, offered to will her estate of $2 million to her hometown—but only if officials named a street after her, hung her favorite art in the mayor's office, and agreed to sell her house only to Parisians.

SAND HOTEL ■ In the summer of 2008, a hotel opened in the English seaside resort of Weymouth, Dorset, that was made entirely from sand. A team of four sculptors worked 14 hours a day for a week to build the beach structure from 1,102 tons of sand. For $20 a night, guests could sleep on sand beds in either a twin or double bedroom and gaze at the stars—until the rain washed it all away.

SECRET CASTLE ■ Farmer Robert Fidler from the town of Redhill in Surrey, England, hid a mock Tudor castle behind 40-ft-high (12-m) hay bales for more than four years. After the local council blocked Fidler's plans to build his dream home in one of his fields, the determined farmer erected the disguise from hundreds of bales of straw, topped with huge tarpaulins. He moved his family into the completed castle in 2002, but did not remove the straw façade until four years later in 2006.

TOWN RELOCATION ■ The town of Lynn Lake, Manitoba, Canada, was created in the 1950s by dragging 208 buildings on sleds 93 mi (150 km) from the town of Sherridon.

FOUNTAIN HOTEL ■ In 2007, Japanese artist Tatzu Nishi built a temporary hotel around a fountain in the center of the city of Nantes, France. The Hotel Place Royale consisted of a bedroom with bathroom that was 1,400 sq ft (130 sq m) and enclosed the upper part of the square's famous 19th-century fountain.

UNDERGROUND TEMPLES ■ Members of the Damanhur religious organization in northern Italy have spent decades carving out thousands of cubic feet of earth to build a five-story underground complex, complete with nine temples.

OPTIONAL EXTRA ■ After trying in vain for a year to sell her four-bedroom home in West Palm Beach, Florida, 42-year-old Deven Trabosh came up with a novel method of attracting interest in the property—by including herself in the asking price. Looking for love, the single mother, who had been divorced for 12 years, listed the home for $340,000 on a sell-it-yourself website, but increased the asking price to $840,000 if the buyer decided to take her as part of the package.

The ground gave way under houses in Guatemala City, Guatemala, in February 2007. A sinkhole formed when broken water pipes washed underground soil away, leaving a void that collapsed, causing the death of three people and swallowing at least 12 houses. The resulting hole was more than 200 ft (61 m) deep and 65 ft (20 m) wide.

This vast pit, a diamond mine, is located south of the Arctic Circle in Canada's Northwest Territories. The hole is actually located on an island, and is so remote that it has its own airport. When the surrounding water freezes over in the winter, a supply road is opened up—usable for just two months of the year—which stretches 600 km (372 mi) over frozen lakes to the mine.

A Whole Lot of Holes

One of the biggest manmade holes in the world, the Mir diamond mine in Russia, dominates the nearby town of Mirny, which sits perched on the edge of a 1,722-ft (525-m) drop. The mine is an incredible 3,937 ft (1200 m) in diameter, equivalent to 12 soccer fields lying end to end. It was Russia's biggest source of diamonds, and is so deep that it takes mining trucks more than two hours to get to the bottom of the hole.

With a diameter of 1,519 ft (463 m) and a surface area the size of 225 baseball fields, it's easy to see how the "Big Hole" in Kimberley, South Africa, got its name. Originally a large hill, 50,000 diamond miners worked with pickaxes and shovels from 1866 to 1914 to dig 2,625 ft (800 m)—that's almost half a mile—down into the ground. The hole was then infilled with 115-ft (35-m) of rubble and, later, filled with water to within 130 ft (40 m) of its brim, which leaves a whole lot of hole still under the water!

LIGHTNING STRIKE ■ Kent Lilyerd from Mora, Minnesota, was struck on the top of the head by a bolt of lightning in June 2008—and lived to tell the tale. The bolt knocked him out on his lawn for an hour, but when he came round, he had nothing worse than a small head wound. He was saved by the three layers of wet clothing he was wearing, because the bolt, which also caused a hunting bullet in his pocket to explode, charged through his drenched clothing instead of through his vital organs and exited through his boot's steel toe.

MOVING CRUST ■ In addition to causing tides at sea, the Moon's gravity moves the Earth's crust up and down by up to 12 in (30 cm).

GREEN LAND ■ D.N.A. collected from beneath half a mile (800 m) of ice in Greenland reveals that 500,000 years ago the island really was green. The D.N.A. shows that Greenland was once covered by lush forests of spruce, pine, and yew, which were filled with butterflies, moths, and the ancestors of beetles, flies, and spiders.

FIERY SKY ■ In Sussex, England, in 1958, nearly 2,000 flashes of lightning were recorded in just one hour.

BLACK HOLE ■ Sagittarius A, the black hole at the center of the Milky Way, has a mass that is four million times greater than our Sun.

OLD MAN ■ A natural rock formation at Corner Brook, Newfoundland, Canada, resembles a craggy-faced old man and is known as The Old Man in the Mountain.

COLD DESERT ■ The McMurdo Dry Valleys of Antarctica receive fewer than 4 in (10 cm) of snow per year and are the most ice-free places on the continent. The unique conditions in this extreme desert are caused by katabatic winds, which occur when cold, dense air is pulled downhill by the force of gravity. These winds can reach speeds of 200 mph (320 km/h), evaporating all moisture—water, ice, and snow—in the process.

SPACE GRAVITY ■ The Earth's gravity is only about ten percent weaker on the International Space Station, which orbits 200 mi (320 km) up in space, than it is here on the ground.

ROCK OF AGES ■ The Nuvvuagittuq rock belt, on the eastern shores of Hudson Bay, Quebec, Canada, is 4.28 billion years old—almost as old as the Earth itself. Most of the Earth's original surface has been crushed and recycled through the movement of giant tectonic plates, but the Nuvvuagittuq rocks, which have been found to contain ancient volcanic deposits, have survived.

VANISHING ROCK ■ Although the Earth's crust consists of solid rock, if you were to break it down into its component elements, nearly half of it would vanish into thin air, because 46.6 percent of the Earth's crust is made up of oxygen.

FLOATING ROCKS ■ Some rocks can actually float. In the course of a volcanic eruption, the violent separation of gas from lava produces a frothy rock called pumice, which is full of gas bubbles and can float on water.

LONG DRINK ■ It would take a person 143,737,166,324 million years to drink the 2,662 million trillion pints (1,260 million trillion liters) of water on Earth, at a rate of two pints (one liter) per hour and with no bathroom breaks.

LIGHTNING QUICK ■ In a storm, lightning is seen before thunder is heard because light travels faster than sound. The difference between the speed of light and the speed of sound is so great that light could travel around the world before sound finished a 100-m sprint.

POISON LAKE ■ On August 21, 1986, a highly concentrated amount of carbon dioxide bubbled to the surface of Cameroon's Lake Nyos and suffocated 1,746 people and thousands of animals as far as 15 miles away.

LUCKY GIRL ■ Sixteen-year-old BreAnna Helsel survived being struck by lightning at her home in Blanchard, Michigan, in June 2008—and the next day she won $20 in the state lottery.

ICE SHOT

Kenneth Libbrecht from Pasadena, California, is an expert on ice and snow, and takes incredibly detailed photographs of real snowflakes using a specially designed photomicroscope that illuminates the clear flakes with colored lights. The professor of physics braves sub-zero temperatures to catch snowflakes from the air and take photographs in the short time before they melt.

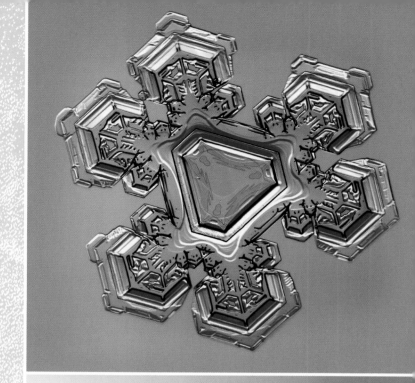

BIKINI REEF ■ A coral reef now thrives in the Pacific atoll of Bikini, where the Castle Bravo, a U.S. thermonuclear test bomb, exploded in 1954. The bomb vaporized three islands, raised water temperatures to 99,000°F (55,000°C), shook islands 125 mi (200 km) away and left a crater more than a mile wide on the ocean floor.

TRANSATLANTIC DUST ■ Some of the dust that blows over Florida has come all the way from Africa. The dust is kicked up by high winds in North Africa and carried to an altitude of 20,000 ft (6,100 m), where it becomes caught up in the trade winds and is transported across the Atlantic. Dust from China also makes its way to North America.

TORNADO TERROR ■ Dan and Jennifer Wells of Northmoor, Missouri, were married in Kansas City in 2003 three days after a tornado completely destroyed their home—Jennifer's wedding dress, hanging in a nearby shed, was untouched.

WHITE RAIN ■ On January 7, 2008, a white-colored rain fell across Grant and Catron counties in New Mexico. The strange rain, which contained high levels of calcium and left milky puddles and a milky white residue over a large area, was thought to have been caused by lake-bed dust from a dry lake in Arizona. The dust particles may have penetrated the clouds and fallen as rain.

DISTANT SHOCK ■ In 1985, a swimming pool at the University of Arizona in Tucson lost water from sloshing caused by the Michoacan earthquake taking place 1,240 mi (1,995 km) away in Mexico.

TORNADO TUESDAY ■ Eighty seven tornadoes combined to devastate areas of five U.S. states—Arkansas, Tennessee, Kentucky, Mississippi, and Alabama—on "Super Tuesday," February 5–6, 2008. Two of the tornadoes had wind speeds of up to 200 mph (320 km/h) and the storms created hailstones as big as softballs—around 4½ in (11.4 cm) in diameter.

TRAVELER'S TREE ■ Thirsty travelers in Madagascar need only pierce the thick end of the leaf stalk of the tropical plant *Ravenala madagascariensis* to obtain plenty of water. Owing to its unusual leaf formation, with a vessel-like shape at the base of each stalk, a single specimen of the traveler's tree, as it is popularly known, can store up to 2½ pt (1.2 l) of water.

WATER SUPPLY ■ A newly discovered Mexican plant species has no chlorophyll and gets all its water and nutrients from the trees on which it feeds.

SUBWAY FLOODS? ■ Even in dry weather, the New York City subway system pumps out ten million gallons of water a day. Scientists say that owing to rising sea levels caused by global warming, the city's subways could be completely flooded by the end of the century.

SOLE DEATH ■ Around 500 meteorites, ranging in size from marbles to basketballs, hit the surface of Earth each year—but the only reported fatality over the past 100 years was a dog that was hit by one in Egypt in 1911.

FLYING BABY ■ In February 2008, a tornado in Castalian Springs, Tennessee, ripped 11-month-old Kyson Stowell from his mother's arms and threw him 400 ft (120 m) into a muddy field—where he was found alive and healthy. He was discovered among a collection of plastic dolls that had been picked up by the twister as it destroyed a nearby house.

LIGHTNING MAGNET ■ The Empire State Building in New York is struck by lightning some 500 times a year. It was once hit 12 times in 20 minutes, disproving the theory that lightning never strikes twice in the same place.

BURNED BUTT ■ In October 2006, Natasha Timarovic of Zadar, Croatia, survived a lightning strike to her mouth as she brushed her teeth. She was saved because she was wearing rubber-soled bathroom shoes, so instead of grounding through her feet, the electricity shot out of her backside, miraculously leaving her with only minor burns to her body.

MOVING CLOSER ■ Los Angeles, California, is moving toward San Francisco, also in California, at a rate of about 2 in (5 cm) a year, because the San Andreas Fault, which runs north–south, is slipping. Scientists predict that Los Angeles will be a suburb of San Francisco in around 15 million years.

VAST VOLCANO ■ The Olympus Mons volcano on Mars rises 16 mi (26 km) into the Martian sky, its base being so big that it would cover nearly the whole of Arizona.

GHOST ORCHID ■ The Ghost Orchid has no leaves and no stem. When it isn't flowering, the plant is just a system of roots.

BLACK HOLE ■ Located 3.5 billion light years away from Earth, OJ287, the largest black hole ever discovered, has a mass equivalent to 18 billion Suns.

TREE MOVE ■ To save a 750-year-old boab tree from becoming a casualty of a road-widening scheme, Australian Aboriginals arranged for it to be uprooted from its home in Western Australia in 2008 and moved a distance of 1,900 mi (3,060 km) by truck with a police escort to a park in the state capital Perth. The bottle-shaped tree, which has religious significance to the local people, stands 46 ft (14 m) high, measures 8 ft (2.4 m) in diameter, and weighs around 36 tons. Boabs can live for up to 2,000 years.

MOON LAKE ■ A newly discovered lake at the south pole of Saturn's largest moon Titan is bigger than Lake Ontario. Covering an area of 7,800 sq mi (20,200 sq km), the lake is filled mostly with methane and ethane, which are gases on Earth, but liquids on the ice-cold surface of Titan.

FAST FRONT ■ A cold weather front can move at speeds of up to 30 mph (48 km/h)—faster than Olympic sprinters can run.

METEORITE HUNTER ■ Steve Arnold of Kingston, Arkansas, has dug up more than 1,000 meteorites in 15 years of searching. In 2005, he found one in Kiowa County, Kansas, that weighed nearly three-quarters of a ton.

ZAP CHAP! ■ Peter McCamphill of Warwickshire, England, survived a lightning strike in 2007 that burned off his hair, blackened his clothes, and tore one of his shoes into pieces.

SAFEST STATES ■ Between 1975 and 1995, there were only four U.S. states that did not have any earthquakes—Florida, Iowa, North Dakota, and Wisconsin.

FLASHLIGHT DIG ■ Trapped beneath 20 ft (6 m) of snow from an avalanche near Ouray, Colorado, it took Danny Jaramillo 18 hours to dig his way to safety—using a flashlight as a shovel.

Ripley's research

Swimmers in the "Devil's Pool" are protected by a naturally formed rock wall, which enables them to bathe quite safely, literally on the edge of Victoria Falls. However, it is safe to do so only between the months of September and January, when the flow of water over the falls is at its lightest—at other times of the year bathers risk being washed over the edge into the abyss.

The Devil's Swimming Pool

Possibly the most dangerous swimming pool in the world, the "devil's pool," as it is known, is a dip in the rocks found on the very edge of Victoria Falls on the Zambezi River in Africa. Local guides lead tourists to the pool on the Zambian side of the falls, where it is possible to bathe only inches from a terrifying 328-ft (100-m) drop, despite a fast-moving current and the vast volume of water that rushes over the falls.

Index

Page numbers in *italics* refer to illustrations

ACKNOWLEDGMENTS

COVER (l) mauisurfboardfence.com/photographer: John Hugg huggsmaui.com, (t/r) Dan Burton www.underwaterimages.co.uk, (b/r) Pooktre; BACK COVER Ashley Bradford; 4 Ray Asgar www.austinhelijet.com; 6–7 © CERN; 8 (t) Alan Blacklock NIWA; 8–9 (b) Eric Gay/AP/PA Photos; 9 Lori Mehmen/AP/PA Photos; 10–11 Bill Counsell; 12 (b) Pooktre; 12–13 (t) Phil Yeomans/Rex Features; 13 (b) ChinaFotoPress/ Photocome/PA Photos; 14 (t) NASA, NOAO, ESA, the Hubble Helix Nebula Team, M. Meixner (STScI), and T.A. Rector (NRAO), (b) NASA and The Hubble Heritage Team (STScI/AURA); 14–15 (dp) NASA and The Hubble Heritage Team (AURA/STScI); 15 (t) Credit for Hubble Image: NASA, ESA, K. Kuntz (JHU), F. Bresolin (University of Hawaii), J. Trauger (Jet Propulsion Lab), J. Mould (NOAO), Y.-H. Chu (University of Illinois, Urbana), and STScI. Credit for CFHT Image: Canada-France-Hawaii Telescope/ J.-C. Cuillandre/Coelum. Credit for NOAO Image: G. Jacoby, B. Bohannan, M. Hanna/ NOAO/AURA/NSF, (b) NASA, ESA, HEIC, and The Hubble Heritage Team (STScI/AURA). knowledgment: R. Corradi (Isaac Newton Group of Telescopes, Spain) and Z. Tsvetanov (NASA); 16 (t, b/r) Steve Nicol/Australian Antarctic Division, (b/l) Barcroft Media; 17 Steve Nicol/Australian Antarctic Division; 19 © Joseph Sohm/Visions of America/Corbis; 20–21 Dan Burton www.underwaterimages.co.uk; 22 (t) Bournemouth News & Pic Service/Rex Features; 22–23 (b) Reuters/Ho New; 23 (t) Dave Thompson/ PA Wire/PA Photos; 24 mauisurfboardfence.com/photographer: John Hugg huggsmaui.com; 25 Zoom/Barcroft Media; 26 (t) Kirk Lee Aeder/ Barcroft Media, (b) Peter Willows/Rex Features; 26–27 (dp) Newspix/David Sheridan/Rex Features; 28 (t) Ray Asgar www.austinhelijet.com, (b) Ashley Bradford; 29 Frank Hormann/AP/PA Photos; 30 (t/l) © Ulises Rodriguez/epa/Corbis, (t/r) © Cameron French/Reuters/Corbis, (b/l) Reuters/Sergei Karpukhin, (b/r) Heinrich van den Berg/Getty Images; 31 Kenneth Libbrecht/Barcroft Media; 33 (sp) Francisc Stugren, (t) Photoshot/Imagebroker.net

Key: t = top, b = bottom, c = center, l = left, r = right, sp = single page, dp = double page

All other photos are from Ripley Entertainment Inc.
Every attempt has been made to acknowledge correctly and contact copyright holders and we apologize in advance for any unintentional errors or omissions, which will be corrected in future editions.